Visit us on the Web! www.randomhouse.com/kids

Educators and librarians, for a variety of teaching tools, visit us at
www.randomhouse.com/teachers

Library of Congress Cataloging-in-Publication Data is available upon request.
ISBN 978-0-375-86926-6 (trade) — ISBN 978-0-375-96926-3 (lib. bdg.)

MANUFACTURED IN CHINA

10 9 8 7 6 5 4 3 2 1

First Edition

The Bunny's Night-Light

A Glow-in-the-Dark Search

GEOFFREY HAYES

Random House 🏠 New York

"Papa," said Bunny, "I can't sleep. There's too much dark at night."

Papa said to Bunny, "You need a night-light."

The moon was sailing in her gown of clouds.

"Maybe the moon can be your night-light," said Papa.

But Bunny said, "No. The moon is too *bright* to be my night-light."

Stars were twinkling in the deep
black sky.

"Pretty as your twinkling eyes," said Papa.
"Maybe the stars can be your night-light."

But Bunny said, "No. The stars are too *twinkly* to be a good night-light for me."

Bunny and Papa found fireflies dancing over the lettuce field, busy being busy.

"Fireflies?" asked Papa.

"Too *busy*," said Bunny.

Bunny found a little glowworm.

But it could not be Bunny's night-light.

It was already its own night-light.

Papa found another light on a boat on the water. He sang:

"The fisherman hums in the quiet night,
safe on his boat in his lantern's light."

Bunny said, "That light is almost too *small* for me to see."

"True," said Papa. "Still, it's nice to know it's there."

House lights, porch lights, streetlights—all
kinds of lights—glowed in the warm night . . .

. . . and in the rabbit town.

"Look, Bunny," said Papa. "The night is filled with light!"

Bunny sighed. "I know. But we still haven't found a light for me."

"I don't suppose you'd consider a
streetlight?" Papa asked.

"Papa," said Bunny. "Be serious. That light
is too *tall* to fit in my room!"

Papa scratched his ear. "Oh, you want a
light for your room? Well, of course you do.
I must have dust bunnies on the brain! Let's
go ask Mama."

So Papa and Bunny went to their cozy
rabbit home to ask Mama if she knew of a
night-light for Bunny.

"That's easy," said Mama. "Grandma gave
me a night-light when I was a little girl, and I
believe I know just where to find it."

Papa and Bunny followed Mama to the
back of the house, down a wooden stair,
where, close among the beetroots in the
warm earth, there was a little door.

Inside the door was a little room.
Inside the room was a little box.
Inside the box was a little lamp.

It wasn't too busy, it wasn't too small.
It wasn't too twinkly, too bright, or too tall.

And it made wonderful shadows of ships
on the wall!

"Oh, Mama, Papa, thank you!" cried Bunny.
"This light is perfect!"

The little boats rock on the water,
Shadow ships sail through the air.
And bunnies can sleep
Through the darkening deep
Of the night without a care;
For there's always a light somewhere.
There's always a light somewhere.

Good night.